Pecky Pe
and Friends

Danger at Pinnacle Point

Tom Isabella and Chris Isabella
Illustrations by: Matt Jaco

outskirts press

Outskirts Press, Inc.
http://www.outskirtspress.com

ISBN: 978-1-9772-4186-3

Outskirts Press and the "OP" logo are trademarks belonging to Outskirts Press, Inc.

PRINTED IN THE UNITED STATES OF AMERICA

Dedication

Tom Isabella would like to dedicate this book to all of those who remain young at heart, and those who take risks to follow their dreams.

Matthew Jaco would like to dedicate this book to his parents for putting him through art classes growing up and to his children to show them that, no matter how old you get, continue to pursue your passion in life.

Christopher Isabella would like to dedicate this book to Kayla, Jackson, and Aubrey who teach him that there are always new things to learn and that every stage in life is a wonderful new adventure.

Pecky Penguin was a very peculiar penguin. He was tall and skinny rather than short like all his cousins. Pecky's long pants weren't very long because he was so tall. In fact, they were more like shorts! He also wore glasses which was very rare for a Penguin. Did Pecky like swimming? No, he did not. Did he like fish? No, he liked spaghetti instead. His mom always joked that he was not really a penguin.

Pecky was smart, and he liked reading books, but he didn't like school much because he didn't have many friends. His mom had to make him go each morning and sometimes he got to school late. After each day, she would ask him if he had made any friends. He would always answer "no". The summer break was almost over, and Pecky said to himself that this school year would be different. He was going to make a new friend!

Pecky had one more day before school started. He wanted to do something fun, but his mom, and dad were too busy to play with him. So Pecky decided to take a walk to the playground.

Pecky started walking but took a wrong turn. He ended up in Polar Bear Alley by mistake! Pecky's dad told him to never go there. He turned around and tried to leave but bumped into something hard with a loud "thud"! Pecky looked up to see a huge polar bear standing behind him.

The polar bear was wearing red polka dot shorts and a blue shirt with pink flowers. He had a large grin on his face when he said, "Hi! I'm Peter." Pecky looked at him and said, "Um, I'm Pecky. Please don't eat me." Peter said, "I would never eat you! I like spaghetti. What are you doing here?"

"I think I took a wrong turn," said Pecky. "I was going to the playground." Well, it turned out to be Pecky's lucky day, because Peter looked at him and said, "I happen to be going there too. Do you skateboard?" "Oh no!", exclaimed Pecky. "I might get hurt!" Peter laughed and told Pecky to climb on his back. Away they went!

When they got to the playground, they found a group of kids playing. Peter went right up to them and said, "Hello I'm Peter!". Pecky turned red and hid behind Peter. Petunia the penguin, Sammy the seal, and Fanny the fox all loudly said, "Hi" and quickly invited Peter and Pecky to play with them. After a while, they got bored, and Peter said, "I sure would like to go swimming". Pecky said, "Oh Peter, we don't have to go swimming, let's do something else", because Pecky did not like to swim. Petunia said, "I would like to go swimming too. Sammy said, "what is the matter Pecky are you afraid to go swimming"? Pecky said, "no, I just want to do something else".

Fanny said, "I know the perfect place to swim. It is called Pinnacle Point." Pecky said, "My mom always said not to go near Pinnacle Point because there have been sharks seen there, and they could eat us." Petunia said, "Pecky is right. My daddy said if I went there, I would be in trouble." Sammy said, "I think that anyone who doesn't go swimming at Pinnacle Point is a big chicken." Petunia asked, "What is a chicken?". Sammy answered, "I am not sure, but my dad calls me that sometimes when I am scared to do something." Peter said, "Well I am not scared, and I am no chicken. I will swim anywhere I want to." Petunia said, "Well, I guess I am not afraid either", but she did not seem sure.

Sammy said, "ok everyone, go home and get your swimming gear and meet us at Pinnacle Point, and remember don't tell your mom or dad, because it is a secret". Peter and Sammy seemed excited, but Pecky, Petunia, and Fanny were scared. No one wanted to seem scared, so they all said they would meet.

When Peter got home his mom Paula was cooking lunch. Peter tried to run upstairs and grab his swimming gear, but his mom insisted he have lunch! Of course, a polar bear would need a big lunch! Paula asked what he was doing. Peter was so excited he forgot about the secret and said, "me and all of my friends are going to Pinnacle Point to go swimming", but he knew he had messed up and said, "OOPS". Paula quickly told Peter's dad and they decided to call all the other kid's parents and to meet at Pinnacle Point.

In the meantime, all the friends except Peter were at Pinnacle Point. Pecky said, "I wonder what happened to Peter?" Sammy said, "don't worry about that silly bear come on let's get in the water." They all jumped in the water and started to play. While they were swimming and playing Pecky noticed that the water started splashing and loud slapping sounds were getting closer to him and his friends.

Suddenly, Pecky saw the fin of a shark come out of the water. Pecky yelled "SHARK swim for the beach, hurry".

All the friends were swimming as hard and fast as they could but Pecky was the slowest and the shark was gaining on him. He could feel the shark just behind him almost touching his tail.

Pecky's dad Paul and his mom Patty, and the other parents got to Pinnacle Point and saw what was happening. Paul said, "come on let's save our children." They all swam past the children straight for the shark. The parents started splashing and yelling as loud as they could, and Paul the penguin even hit the shark in the nose. The shark was confused, and he knew he couldn't fight all of the parents, so he gave up and swam away. The parents helped their children back to the beach. Everyone was tired but happy to be safe.

Later that evening everyone met at Peter's home and Peter said, "I am sorry for telling our secret, it just slipped out." Pecky's dad said, "it is a good thing you did because your friends could have been eaten." Petunia's, dad Philip asked the other children, "Why did you go to Pinnacle Point when you knew it was dangerous?" Pecky said, "We knew it was wrong, but Sammy kept saying if we did not go, then we were chickens."

Pecky's dad cleared his throat and said, "Well, I guess we have all learned something today. We should not do things that are dangerous or wrong because someone calls us names or dares us." "We should not lie or keep secrets because someone might get hurt if we do." Everyone nodded and agreed. Not only did Pecky make new friends that day, but he also learned a valuable lesson.

Biographies

Tom Isabella is a retired analyst for the Federal Bureau of Investigation and holds a Master of Arts in Communications Degree from West Virginia University. His passions are travel, photography, reading, chess, volunteering, and art. He resides in White Hall, West Virginia with his partner Brenda Cain.

Matthew Jaco is an engineer in the Natural Gas industry who holds a bachelor's degree in Civil Engineering from Fairmont State University in West Virginia. His passions are spending time with his family, traveling, sports, riding motorcycles, golfing, and doing artwork. He resides in Mount Juliet, Tennessee with his wife Alexandria, son Zane, and daughter Eliza.

Christopher Isabella is a pharmacist working in the pharmaceutical industry who holds a Doctor of Pharmacy Degree from West Virginia University. His passions include family, traveling around the world, and enjoying the little things in life. He resides in Morgantown, West Virginia with his wife Kayla, son Jackson, and daughter Aubrey.